ARABIAN
STAR

STACEY INTERNATIONAL

Dedication
For Brian – who asks the right questions –
with my love and thanks, Julia

Arabian Star
published by
Stacey International
128 Kensington Church Street
London W8 4BH
Tel: +44(0)20 7221 7166   Fax: +44(0)20 7792 9288
E-mail: info@stacey-international.co.uk
www.stacey-international.co.uk

ISBN: 978 1905 299843
CIP Data: A catalogue record for this book is available from the British Library

Text © Julia Johnson 2009
Illustrations © Henry Climent 2009

1 3 5 7 9 0 8 6 4 2

Printing & Binding: Oriental Press, UAE

Acknowledgements
The author would like to thank several individuals central to the creation of this story:
Captain Stefano and the crew of the *Gemini Star*, particularly Andy and Stanko
and of course Abdulkareem Al Babtain who showed me round and
provided so much information.

The publishers would like to thank
Vela International Marine Limited
without whose kind support this book would not have been possible.

ARABIAN STAR

Story by Julia Johnson

Illustrations by Henry Climent

The turtle was lying in the sand by the water's edge. From a distance its domed shell could easily be mistaken for a rock. The boy shielded his eyes against the bright sunlight. His heart was pounding as he ran.

It was a green turtle, he recognised it from its markings. And then he saw the chip in its shell. Only yesterday he had dived beneath the waves and watched it swim along the edge of the reef, feeding on sea grasses. Several nights ago he had secretly watched this turtle lumber up the beach, laboriously dig a hole and lay her eggs.

Now her head lolled forwards, limp and lifeless.

The boy reached out and stroked a leathery flipper. He examined the body for damage. Had she become entangled in a fishing net and drowned? Was she a victim of an oil spill? Had she been attacked by a shark? But there were no obvious signs. Perhaps she had swallowed a plastic bag, mistaking it for a jellyfish. Threats to turtles were numerous, he knew.

Angrily he rubbed his eyes and jumped up.

The raft was as good as finished. He had made it well, lashing the wooden slats firmly together. His father had shown him how to tie the ropes securely with special knots. He hadn't tested the raft yet, but now seemed as good a time as any. It lay propped against the shelter of palm fronds.

Dragging it down to the water's edge, he wedged it into the sand so that it would not be able to float away until he was ready. Carefully he scraped away some sand from under the turtle until he had made a hollow. Then he found a plank of wood and manoeuvred it into position beneath the creature so that he could lift and slide its body onto the raft.

The turtle was big and heavy, and it was hard work, but the boy was determined to return her to the sea where she belonged. He hated the thought of gulls screeching and fighting over her flesh. He stretched a length of rope around the turtle and fixed it to the raft so that she would not fall into the water too soon.

He watched the white lip of foam lap at the edge of the raft and gradually lift it. He pushed the raft until he was standing waist deep, and then he hauled himself aboard and began to paddle the raft over the rise and fall of the incoming tide.

For some time he concentrated on paddling, aware that if he stopped the sea's current might cause him to drift towards the shore again.

A gentle breeze began to blow, and he no longer needed to paddle so hard. He was pleased with the raft. It would be even better, he thought, if he secured some empty oil drums to the underside. That way he would be raised above the waves and the sea wouldn't be able to slop over its surface. He might make a mast and a sail for it as well.

The boy glanced back at the shoreline and was surprised to see how far away it looked. He could barely make out the shape of the palm frond shelter. He had better do what he had set out to do and head home. Quickly he untied the rope securing the turtle. Pushing her towards the edge of the raft, he said a prayer and slid her overboard. The raft tilted precariously and the boy was in danger of being washed into the sea with the turtle. He gasped as water hit him in the face, but he held on tight until the raft was steady again, and then he began to paddle towards the shore.

His arms felt tired now, and the tide had turned. No matter how hard he paddled the shoreline did not seem to be getting any closer. The breeze was growing stronger too. He wished he had talked to his father, he would have come with him, and now, instead of drifting out to sea on a raft, he would be sitting in his father's fishing boat and they would have an engine to speed them home. His father would be cross when he discovered what a stupid thing he had done. "Never go out to sea alone," he had warned him, "and always make sure that someone on shore knows." But the boy had been upset. His anger had got the better of him. He had allowed it to rule him, to make him act hastily without thinking, and now he was paying the price.

The Captain of the tanker was feeling pleased with his crew. Although it was an enormous ship there were only 26 men on board and each man had an important job to do, from the lowliest ordinary seaman to the highest ranking Chief Officer and Chief Engineer. They had made good time; in fact they were ahead of schedule, the Captain thought with satisfaction.

Sailing through the Mediterranean Sea the Egyptian coastline should come into view before long. When they reached Suez on the Red Sea in about three days time there would be a partial change of crew,

and the Captain was looking forward to his shore leave. Four months is a long time to be at sea, but soon he would see his family again. He pictured his baby daughter. She had just learnt to crawl when he left. Would she recognize him, he wondered, and laugh when he tickled her the way she used to do? He studied himself in the mirror as he trimmed his beard. Tomorrow or the next day he would shave it off in preparation for his homecoming. His wife Mariam did not care for prickly whiskers!

His thoughts turned to his son. Malik had grown taller, "He hopes he will reach your shoulder," Mariam had written in an email to him.

She had sent a picture, but that was nothing compared to seeing his son with his own eyes! Malik would have so much to tell him and so much to show him. He was doing well at school, Mariam had said, and was showing an aptitude for science and maths. That was good, especially if he wanted to become a seaman like his father. He liked drawing too. Perhaps he would work in the research department and design ships of the future.

The rest of the crew were probably imagining their homecomings too, the Captain thought. All over the world they would be reunited with their families. There was an interesting mix of nationalities on board, men from Poland and Croatia, from India and the Philippines, from Britain and Italy, and of course he himself from Saudi Arabia. The chef had been hard tested to cater for so many different tastes, but he had created some imaginative dishes, and the men, for the most part, had enjoyed his offerings.

The Captain wondered how many of the men would stay in touch. Many of them would probably meet again on future voyages. Some had made firm friendships, others were loners who were quite happy with their own company, and that was not a bad thing, the Captain reflected, when isolated from the rest of society for long periods of time.

However, everyone had enjoyed the occasions when the whole crew had got together. He remembered the karaoke night when the Filipinos had entertained everyone, impressing the others with their impersonations of famous singers. There had been thunderous applause for the third engineer, looking just like Elvis in one of the ship's white boiler suits, padded at the shoulders and decorated with stars. Round his middle he had worn a wide belt with a big brass buckle which the bosun had made in his workshop, and his black hair was flicked up into a cowlick, his hips gyrating for all he was worth! The Captain smiled as he remembered.

Suddenly his thoughts were interrupted by his telephone ringing. "Weather warning, Sir," the Chief Officer announced. Quickly the Captain left his cabin and hurried up to the bridge, where he read the forecast from the meteorological office coming through on the computer screen. "So a fierce squall is expected, is it?" mused the Captain. But he was not worried. A tanker was one of the safest ships on the seas. Its immense size made it extremely stable, and besides it was well maintained – his Chief Engineer made sure of that. Machinery and parts were constantly being checked and changed before things could go wrong.

Anyway a squall was usually over and done with in a matter of minutes, unlike the storm which had hit them off the coast of South Africa. Now that really was a storm, a storm of almost hurricane proportions. A wild and howling wind had whipped the waves into a

fury, bright flashes of lightning illuminated the sea, and the thunder growled like an angry monster all night, the Captain remembered. Some of the crew were afraid, but the tanker was built to withstand a storm, no matter how violent, and though it rolled from side to side it was never in any danger of capsizing.

The boy was growing weary, and did not think he would be able to hold on much longer. His little raft, which he had thought so strong, could not withstand the force of the wind and the waves, and was rapidly being ripped apart. The boy clung desperately to a remaining plank of wood, his knuckles almost white with the effort. He was soaking wet and the wind made him shiver. He felt sick with fear.

An enormous wave engulfed the boy, dragging the wood from under him. He was hurled over and over until he had no idea which way up he was. He felt himself being sucked down into a whirling mass of water. Water was in his eyes, his ears, his nose, his throat. With every last ounce of strength he fought his way to the surface. Coughing and spluttering he emerged at last, struggling for breath, gulping in air. Frantically he searched for the piece of wood. There it was just ahead of him. It looked so close, but every time it seemed within his reach a wave would toss it away again. At last he managed to grab hold of the rope trailing from the piece of wood, and by pulling it through his hands he gradually succeeded in drawing the plank closer and closer until he was able to haul himself onto it.

As suddenly as it had started the squall died. The boy lay face down on the wooden plank, utterly exhausted.

The Captain was relieved that the squall was quickly over. He did not want to be delayed on this last stretch of his voyage. But just as he was thinking this, the ship's Third Officer called out, "Look Captain, a distress signal is coming through!" For a moment the Captain was irritated. Sometimes distress signals came from small yachts with crews who had taken unnecessary risks. When they found themselves in trouble they expected other seamen to risk their lives to rescue them. The Captain banished such an uncharitable thought, reminding himself that no-one wanted to abandon a treasured boat unless he really had to. Safety of life at sea was the most important thing and ships had a duty to help those in distress if they were in the area – that was the law of the sea.

The Captain looked at the details coming in from the coastguard and read with growing alarm. This was not a yacht in distress but a young boy, ten years old, the same age as his beloved son Malik. Apparently the boy had gone out on a home-made raft early that morning and had not been seen since. "What on earth did he do a stupid thing like that for?" the Captain said angrily, trying to hide his concern. "Probably day-dreaming and drifted out to sea when the tide turned," the Third Officer suggested. "The coastguard was alerted by the boy's father when he discovered his son's raft was missing. He will have been caught in the squall sir," he added.

The Captain looked at his watch, it was almost three in the afternoon, the boy might have been in the water for several hours by now. And how were they going to find him? It would be like looking for a needle in a haystack. The boy did not have a radio so they would not be able to establish contact with him. The radar equipment would not register him because he was too small. They could be in danger of sailing right over the top of the boy without ever realizing they had done so. The bridge deck was at least thirty metres above the sea, and looking over the side, it was impossible to see everything below. They could not even plot his position on the chart, although the Captain reckoned he could make a rough estimate if he took into account the tidal flow from the boy's point of departure, the wind speed and the approximate speed a simple wooden raft might travel in such conditions.

The only reliable piece of information they had was that the boy was wearing a red T-shirt. Well at least that was something, the Captain thought, always supposing he was still wearing it of course. There was one other thing which just might help…

The Captain called his officers together and immediately gave the command to slow the ship. Three of the crew were ordered to man one of the two lifeboats in preparation for a possible rescue. If they were lucky enough to spot the boy the ship would not be able to come to a complete halt straight away. It would take a long time to stop a vessel this size, and by then they would be well past the boy and might not find him again. A lifeboat was their only chance.

Two of the officers, one on each of the outer arms of the bridge, scanned the water with binoculars.

And the last thing… the Captain trained his own binoculars on the top of the foremast, three hundred metres away at the front of the deck. Sure enough a large black crow was perched on top of it, just as he had hoped…

Afloat on his piece of wood, the boy opened his eyes. His lips were parched and cracked and salty and he longed for a drink of water. His body felt bruised all over from the sea's battering. Raising his head slowly he looked around. There was no sign of land in any direction and the sea stretched away endlessly all around him. Above him a weak and watery sun filtered through a pale, cloudy sky. There was no wind now, no cry of a gull, no sound at all, save for the gentle slap of the sea against the wooden plank.

His father had taught him how to tell the time of day by the position of the sun in the sky. He calculated that it must be late afternoon. Darkness would fall soon, and then there would be little chance of rescue. He wondered how soon the sea would swallow him up. Would his body eventually be washed ashore? Would his parents ever know what had happened to him? At the thought of his parents he felt a lump well up in his throat, and loneliness engulfed him.

The crew of the tanker was growing ever more anxious. The Captain had informed company headquarters of the situation, and everyone agreed that the search should continue whilst there was enough daylight, but even the powerful beams from the ship's searchlights would be unlikely to pick out the small figure of the little boy in the black of night.

Suddenly the harsh shriek of the crow pierced the air! Three pairs of binoculars were instantly trained on the foremast. "Look!" cried the Chief Officer, "The crow is leaving its perch!" Sure enough the crow had spotted something off the ship's starboard side. Could it be the boy? The three men tried to keep the bird in their sights as it flew, but it was becoming a mere speck in the distance and its cry was growing fainter. The Captain scanned the water below the bird, and what he saw made his heart leap!

Three men were already securely strapped in position in the lifeboat, the coxswain at the helm. Quickly the painter, a rope attached to the bow, was untied and the pins released so that the rescue vessel could be launched. It was lowered rapidly into the water. The Captain saw the boat release the hooks, heard the engine start and the little boat sped away in the direction of the crow.

Meanwhile the boy on his plank of wood was drifting in and out of sleep when suddenly his dreams were punctured by a jarring shriek. He blinked and opened his eyes and then he blinked again. He must still be dreaming he thought. He looked up and was startled to see a large black bird squawking loudly just above his head and speeding its way across the water towards him was a small orange boat.

Before he knew it he was being tossed a lifebelt and pulled towards the boat, which had slowed down to almost a standstill. Strong arms reached out to him and lifted him into the boat. One of the men wrapped him in a blanket and gave him water to sip. Nothing had ever tasted so good! He heard a man say "Got him," and another voice answered through the radio system, "Well done! We'll get on to Headquarters right away so that they can inform the boy's parents that their son is safe. How is he, is he alright?" "In pretty good shape, Sir, all things considered," the man replied. "Possibly a bit dehydrated, but that's only to be expected after eight or nine hours in the water."

As the boat picked up speed the boy could make out an enormous shape looming closer and closer. He had never seen anything as huge in all his life. And the bird which had appeared out of nowhere, where had it come from, where had it gone? Perhaps he was dreaming even now and would wake up to find himself still lost at sea. He closed his eyes again and slept.

It was not until late the next morning that the boy at last opened his eyes again. He yawned and stretched. "Good morning, young man, that was a long sleep," said a voice. "Are you feeling better now?" The boy sat up and saw a bearded man in a smart uniform standing in the doorway smiling at him. "Allow me to introduce myself," said the man, "I am Suleiman and I'm the Captain of the *Arabian Star*."

The boy looked round. "Where am I?" he asked. "In the ship's hospital," the Captain answered. "Your raft broke apart in the storm and we managed to rescue you. Another few minutes and you might have drowned." Memories of yesterday's ordeal came flooding back and the boy shuddered. "We've been looking after you here in the hospital quarters, but you are fine now, I can see that, so how about something to eat?" The boy nodded enthusiastically, he suddenly felt starving.

The Captain gave him some overalls and a pair of lace up shoes to put on. "These are the smallest we could find," he said. "You'll have to roll the legs and sleeves up a bit," he added.

When he was dressed the boy followed the Captain up a stairway and into a room where several men were sitting round a table eating a meal. They all stood up and grinned when the boy was led in. "Here's the shipwrecked sailor," announced the Captain. The men made room for the boy at the table. "What's your name son?" one of them asked. "Ali," replied the boy shyly, and then, realizing how lucky he had been, he added, "Thank you for rescuing me."

With eggs and toast and hot sweet tea inside him Ali felt his energy returning. The men wanted to know all the details of his adventure. Ali was hesitant to admit his foolhardiness, he was well aware that his actions must appear reckless to the crew, but he decided to be honest. The men shook their heads. "You were very lucky," one of them said, "If it hadn't been for that crow…"

So he had heard a bird squawking, it hadn't been a dream after all! "Do you always have a crow on board?" he asked. The men laughed! "Sometimes a bird will join us for a day or two when we are still close to land," the Captain told him. "We've had the occasional racing pigeon hitch a ride for a short time. Once rested it'll take off again and continue on its way. But this crow seems to have made friends with the Chief Engineer," he said.

The Chief Engineer, whose name was Jan, smiled. "Yes indeed," he agreed, "And with the bosun too, we feed Sam Crow you see. But long ago, before the days of radar, sailors would often take crows on board. If they couldn't see land in bad weather they would release one of the birds and plot a course in the direction in which it flew because crows always head for land. The crows' cages would be hung high up on the main mast where the lookout stood his watch, and that's why the perch came to be known as the crow's nest!

"Anyway our crow, Sam, joined us off Ras Tanura on the Saudi Arabian coast," he continued. "Every morning I start the day by jogging round the deck of the ship, and every morning Sam is waiting to greet me from the main mast. By the time I reach the midship mast on the starboard side he is there spurring me on. He flies to the foremast just before I reach it and shrieks at me from there. Then he flies to the midship mast on the port side ahead of me and urges me to get a move on. He's a very good coach." Ali smiled, he was enjoying the story.

"Every time we pass close to land we wonder if Sam will leave us," Jan continued, "but he's stayed with us round the Arabian Peninsula, past Africa and the coast of Brazil. We're too big to sail into most ports, either the water isn't deep enough or the berths aren't big enough, so we have to offload our cargo into three or four smaller vessels. We thought that Sam would take a ride on one of these smaller ships in the Gulf of Mexico, but he didn't. We sailed back via Gibraltar and still he stayed on board. Now we're almost back where we started, so very soon the crow will have travelled right round the world!"

"Just as well he was on board," Captain Suleiman added. "Crows are intelligent and curious. From his perch on the foremast he must have spotted you in your red T-shirt Ali, and then he showed us where you were."

When Ali had finished his breakfast the Captain took him up to the bridge. The wheelhouse was a mass of screens and switches and red and green lights. The Captain found what he was looking for and gave Ali the ship's log book and there he read the account of his rescue. "You found me just in time, didn't you," he said.

He put the book down and looked out of the window. Ali could see the deck far below. It was enormous and seemed to go on for ever. "Three football pitches would fit end to end on that deck," the Captain told him. Ali could see a maze of pipes running over the deck in a criss-cross pattern. "What are all those pipes for?" he asked. "Well the yellow pipes are always for foam for fire fighting," the Captain answered, "and of course most of the others are for the oil," and he added "This ship can carry 300,000 tons of oil." "Oil," Ali shouted and recoiled in horror. He couldn't believe that of all the ships in the sea he had been rescued by an oil tanker. Ever since he had found a dead gull on the beach, its wings thick with oil, he had hated the black, sticky substance. It was smelly and leaked from rusty, dirty old ships and polluted the sea, killing the creatures he loved.

"The world would be a very different place without oil, you know Ali," Captain Suleiman said. Yes, a much better place, Ali thought, but he didn't say so. "Have you ever thought of how many things run on fuel made from oil?" the Captain asked. "Your father's fishing boat for instance," he said. "If we didn't have oil we wouldn't be able to ride around in cars and buses, ships and planes. We'd have to travel by donkeys and horses and camels like people used to do in the past."

Ali thought of his grandfather who was going to perform the Hajj and make the holy pilgrimage to Mecca this year. It was an important part of his faith and the duty of every good Muslim to make the pilgrimage at least once in his lifetime. Grandfather had been saving up for a long time. He had shown Ali the two pieces of seamless white cloth that all the pilgrims wore. He had even bought the ticket for his journey. How awful then if there were no petrol to power the bus. Perhaps some of the oil which this tanker carried might even become that very fuel.

Just then there was a knock on the door. The cook appeared carrying a bowl of meat. "We'll go and feed Sam," said the Captain. "I think it's time our crow had a reward, don't you?" Ali nodded.

The Captain gave Ali a hard hat to put on. "We don't want any accidents," he said, and he bent down to re-tie the boy's laces with double knots. On the deck Captain Suleiman told Ali to walk between the yellow lines where the surface was painted with non-slip paint.

Ali was surprised that everything looked so clean. He could not see a sign of oil anywhere. "We carry the crude oil in several tanks below the deck," the Captain told him, as if reading his thoughts. "Most ships have double hulls nowadays to give more protection to the tanks," he went on. "When we want to offload or fill up we attach hoses to these circular doors," he said. The doors were secured with lots of massive bolts, Ali noticed. "We have separate ballast tanks," Captain Suleiman continued. "The ballast is water which is pumped in to keep the ship stable when its cargo tanks are empty," he explained.

"Look over there!" Ali suddenly shouted excitedly. The Captain followed the boy's gaze. "What can you see?" he asked. Ali pointed, "I think it must be a whale," he said. Captain Suleiman peered into the distance. As they drew nearer he saw what Ali had seen. An enormous jet of water sprayed high into the air from the creature's blowhole and they could make out the distinctive shape of a sperm whale's head. "My goodness, you've got sharp eyes," the Captain remarked. It was a magnificent creature, at least 16 metres long. "It's going to dive," Captain Suleiman told Ali, as the whale arched its back. Then the huge tail fin appeared, rising high out of the water, and they watched as the massive creature plunged into the depths below and out of sight. "Well, wasn't that something!" Captain Suleiman said. Ali's eyes were shining.

It was a long walk from one end of the ship to the other. They passed the lifeboat which had rescued Ali, now winched back into place. "I thought lifeboats were open," said Ali. "Why does this one have a roof on it?" he asked. The Captain explained that if the crew had to abandon ship because of a fire the roof would protect the men from burning debris. "There's a sprinkler system so that water can keep the roof cool," he said. They stepped inside the lifeboat and the Captain showed Ali the concentrated food bars and the supply of medicines stowed on board. There was a tank of water too. Everything was ready in case of an emergency.

"Do you often have to rescue people?" Ali asked. "Good gracious no!" the Captain exclaimed, "And boys on homemade rafts are few and far between, thank goodness," he added. Ali looked shamefaced. How stupid he had been he thought. "You are the very first child we've

had on board," Captain Suleiman told him. "The last rescue we carried out was a long time ago," he continued. "Three people in a small yacht had got into trouble in a monsoon storm off the coast of Oman. Of course we didn't have such difficulty finding them because we were able to pick up their distress signal and plot their whereabouts on our radar. We hoisted them aboard in the basket," he said, and he pointed out a contraption consisting of a large ring connected to a smaller ring which was secured to a crane. "They had to abandon their yacht and of course we all presumed it would sink, but apparently it washed up on the shores of India a few weeks later and after a few repairs it was as good as new." The Captain chuckled, "Who would have thought it?" he said.

Turning to Ali he frowned, "But what on earth made you head out to sea all alone?" he asked. "I don't know," Ali muttered, "I was angry. I didn't mean to go far. I suppose I didn't think," he admitted. The Captain looked at him, "On my ship everyone has to think before they act," he said, "Safety is our business, it's in everything we do."

Sam Crow spied them from his perch on the foremast. With a loud caw he flew down to see what they had brought him. Ali set down the bowl and watched, fascinated, as the crow greedily swallowed its contents in seconds! The Filipino bosun, a short muscular man, came out of his workshop to see what all the noise was about.

"Lester," said the Captain, "I think this young man should see the engine room." He turned to Ali, "Would you like that?" The boy nodded enthusiastically, he loved engines. His father was often tinkering with the engine on his fishing boat and sometimes he let Ali help him. "Right then," said the Captain, "Lester will look after you. I must get back to the bridge."

Lester's workshop was clean and tidy. Ali watched him put his tools away. "They are all air-powered," Lester told him, "We have to be especially careful because we carry oil, so we don't allow electricity or naked flames on deck in case of fire." The boy pointed to a big axe, "What's that for?" he asked. "To release ropes quickly in an emergency," Lester told him, "and this wedge here is called the bitter end." He picked up a giant hammer. "A good blow from this," he told Ali, "And the anchor cables would be released, but we would only do that as a last resort." They stepped out of the workshop and Lester showed Ali the anchors. There were two of them, one on the port side and one on the starboard, and they were enormous! "Wait until you see the engine room," said Lester, and he laughed.

He bent to pick up the bowl with which Ali had fed the crow. "Never leave anything lying on the deck," he told the boy, "If it doesn't get lost overboard it may trip someone up and cause an accident," he said. Goodness! There were a lot of things to remember, Ali thought. "You know what the bowl is made of, don't you?" Lester asked. "Yes, it's plastic," Ali answered. "But did you know that plastic comes from oil?" said Lester. Ali didn't. "You'd be surprised just how many things are by-products of oil," Lester continued. "Paints, detergents, fertilizers, even some fabrics and lots of medicines, road surfaces of course, and tar has been used to make boats watertight for hundreds of years." Ali thought he would remember that when he made a new raft.

He followed Lester over the deck. When he looked up he could see the ship's huge blue funnel behind the bridge, and the radar system turning in the breeze. There were two flags flying. Ali pointed to one, "That's my country's flag," he said. "Yes, we're flying the Egyptian flag because we're in Egyptian waters," Lester told him. "and the other one," he went on, "is the Liberian flag because the ship was registered in Liberia."

They passed a sack of sawdust, and Lester explained that it was to absorb any drop of oil which might fall on the deck during pumping manoeuvres. "Don't you let it go into the sea?" asked Ali. Lester looked shocked. "The only thing we throw into the sea is leftover food. We grind it up first. Of course it attracts lots of fish. Sometimes we see huge shoals of tuna or barracuda. If we were not moving so fast we could catch some!"

"Are you on the move all the time?" Ali asked. "Most of the time, yes," Lester answered, "except when we're moored out at sea at offshore oil terminals and sometimes we moor closer to shore for repairs and so that supplies can be brought out to us. But we can be months at sea without ever setting foot on land," he said.

"Do you like working on a tanker?" Ali asked. "It's an important job," Lester replied. "Everyone needs oil, but only a few countries have it, so we have to make sure that oil is transported safely to all the countries in the world," he said. "I've been on countless voyages," he told Ali, "and I love being at sea." "But not in a storm," Ali suggested. "A really big storm can be frightening," Lester agreed, "but I always carry my lucky marble. My father gave it to me when I was a small boy and I wouldn't go on a ship without it." He dug his hand into his pocket. "You'll find that most sailors carry something with them for luck," he said. Then he frowned, "That's odd," he said, "It isn't here, perhaps I left it in the workshop."

By this time they had reached the lift to the engine room. "The engine room is on five floors and we'll go down to the bottom," he told Ali. He gave Ali some ear plugs. "It's very noisy down there," he explained.

As Ali stepped out of the lift he gasped. He was standing in the bottom of the ship in the most enormous room he had ever seen. Everywhere he looked there were gigantic pumps and pistons, massive compressors and fans, colossal turbines and cables, huge valves and

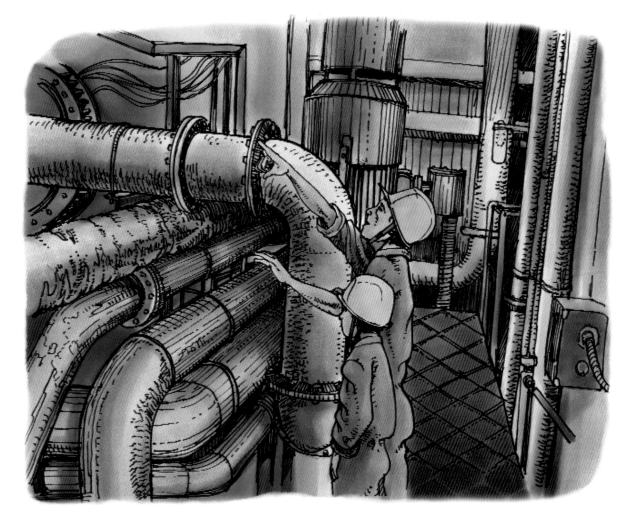

rotors and bearings. Lester pointed to a monstrous shaft which disappeared into the bulkhead, or wall of the ship. "That's the propeller shaft," Lester shouted above the roar of the engine. "The propeller is in the sea on the other side of this bulkhead. All the machinery in here is making the power to turn that shaft which turns the propeller and makes the ship move."

As they stepped back into the lift Lester continued, "The propeller is vast, about five metres across, that's like three men of my height lying head to toe."

They came out into the sunshine again, and Lester picked the boy up and hoisted him onto his shoulders so that Ali could see over the bow. To his delight he could see dolphins leaping over the waves ahead of them. "Dolphins enjoy riding the tanker's bow waves," Lester told him. "When I go out with my father and my uncle in their fishing boat we often see dolphins," Ali said. "Sometimes I dive into the water and the dolphins let me swim with them." "You must be a good swimmer then," Lester said.

"At sea you get to see many things," Lester went on. "I remember once, when I was on another voyage with Captain Suleiman, we were sailing through the Southern Ocean, and an albatross landed on the deck at the bow of the ship. An albatross is a wonderful bird, Ali, with an incredible wingspan. It can wheel and glide over the ocean and cover vast distances. An albatross also has a massive hooked beak and this one was no exception, so the men were afraid to go near it," he went on. "An albatross needs the wind in its wings to take off, but the high sides of the ship meant that there was no air movement, so the bird was stranded," Lester said. "What happened to it?" Ali asked anxiously. "After a few days the Captain decided to try to make friends with it," Lester told him. "He coaxed it with fish, and gradually the bird let him come closer and closer. The Captain was wearing some thick gloves – just in case," said Lester, "but eventually the albatross let him get right up to him, it was as if it knew that the Captain was trying to help him, and it stepped onto his outstretched hands." "And what did the Captain do then?" Ali asked. "He raised the bird slowly up into the air above his head and launched it into the wind," Lester replied, "and do you know before it flew away it circled the ship twice. Then it swooped low and gently brushed the top of the Captain's head with its feet." Lester was silent as he remembered.

"Well, I had better get back to work now," he said. "The Captain wants to see you on the bridge." Ali said goodbye, and called after Lester, "I hope you find your lucky marble."

Captain Suleiman had another surprise for Ali. "Tonight we will be entering the Suez Canal," he told him, "Would you like to stay on board for the journey? Your parents have agreed." "Yes please Sir," Ali replied without hesitation. "Good!" said the Captain, "Then you can disembark with me when we reach Suez."

He picked up a radio phone. Passing it to Ali he said, "There's someone here who would like to speak to you." Ali looked puzzled. "Hello," he said putting his ear to the phone, and then he smiled. "Father," he exclaimed, and for the next few minutes he was busy describing the ship to his father. When he had finished the Captain remarked, "So you think the *Arabian Star* is pretty smart do you? Not a rusty old bath tub after all?" Ali reddened, "I didn't think an oil tanker would be like this," he admitted.

As night approached Ali could see the lights from many ships ahead of them. "They are lining up at Port Said for the convoy through the canal," the Chief Officer told him. "Every ship is given a number and that is its position in the queue," he said.

An Egyptian pilot from the Suez Canal Authority arrived in a tug boat and climbed up the accommodation ladder to board the tanker. He would help guide the ship through the narrow canal. They would steer a course down the middle where the water was deepest. Ali could see the tanker's position on the radar screen.

"We go through partially laden," the Chief Officer said. "When we enter the canal from the other direction we have filled up with oil in Saudi Arabia so we have to off load some of it first through pipes running alongside the canal, and load up again when we reach the

roll-on roll-off   *bulk carrier*

other end," he explained. "If we were full of oil we would be too low in the water and the keel might scrape the bottom," he went on.

He showed Ali a map so that the boy could see how the canal, 190 kilometres of it, linked the Mediterranean Sea to the Gulf of Suez on the Red Sea. "It provides a short cut for ships and means that we don't have to navigate round Africa. We can save about seven days journey time and of course we also save tons of fuel," he explained.

It was getting late and Ali was feeling sleepy. "There won't be much more to see tonight," Captain Suleiman said, "I should get some rest."

The cabin looked cosy and the bed inviting. Ali was soon fast asleep! But he was up again bright and early the next morning, anxious not to miss anything. Hurriedly he pulled on his overalls and thrust his feet into his shoes. Then he remembered the Captain's warning about safety and bent to fasten his shoes up with double knots. He picked up his hard hat and made his way to the bridge where he found Captain Suleiman at his post. He looked the boy up and down and smiled. "Excellent." he said, "We'll make a seaman out of you yet," and he winked at the Chief Officer.

There was something different about the Captain this morning, Ali thought. At first he could not decide what it was. He tried not to stare. Suddenly he realised, "You've shaved off your beard!" he exclaimed. Captain Suleiman chuckled.

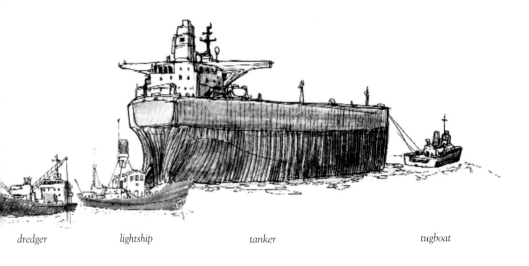

dredger   *lightship*   *tanker*   *tugboat*

Everything seemed very still, and Ali became aware that the tanker was no longer moving. He looked out of the window and saw that they were anchored in a big lake. "Why have we stopped?" he asked. "The canal is single lane only," the Chief Officer replied. "We are moored here in the Bitter Lakes to let the northern convoy through."

Ali went outside. He could see Jan, the Chief Engineer, on his morning run on the deck below. He picked up a pair of binoculars and watched Sam Crow fly from mast to mast ahead of him. As he looked he was surprised to see the bird fly down and land on the deck. Something had captured the crow's attention. Ali could not see what it was from so far away. It looked as if Sam was trying to pick it up, but whatever the object was it kept rolling away from him. Suddenly Ali realized what it was!

When he arrived at Lester's workshop Ali found the bosun looking downcast, but when Ali opened his hand to show him what he'd found a big smile spread across Lester's face. "My lucky marble!" he exclaimed delightedly, "How did you find it?" Ali told him. "I must have lost it during the storm," Lester said, putting it back in his pocket. "What a good thing that you were on board." "And Sam," Ali added. "And Sam," the bosun agreed.

From the bridge Ali watched the ships go past. "That one's known as a Ro-Ro," said the Chief Officer coming up behind him and pointing

to a ship. "A Ro-Ro?" Ali asked. "Yes, a Roll-on Roll-off, it is carrying cars," he answered. "And that one is a bulk carrier," he said, pointing to another. "It's probably carrying grain or steel in its hold." All of the ships were enormous but none of them was as large as the *Arabian Star*.

In the distance Ali could see a ship piled high with containers. "What is that one carrying?" he asked. "Televisions, perhaps, and other electrical goods," the Chief Officer told him, "books, clothes, machinery, all sorts of things," he said. "Ninety percent of the things we have in our homes are brought to us by ships." Ali was amazed. "It looks much too heavy," he declared, but when it drew nearer the Chief Officer pointed out a mark on the ship's side. "That's called the Plimsoll line," he said, "and it shows the point to which the ship can be submerged in water when loaded with cargo. If you could not see that mark then it would be overloaded, but it would not be allowed through the canal."

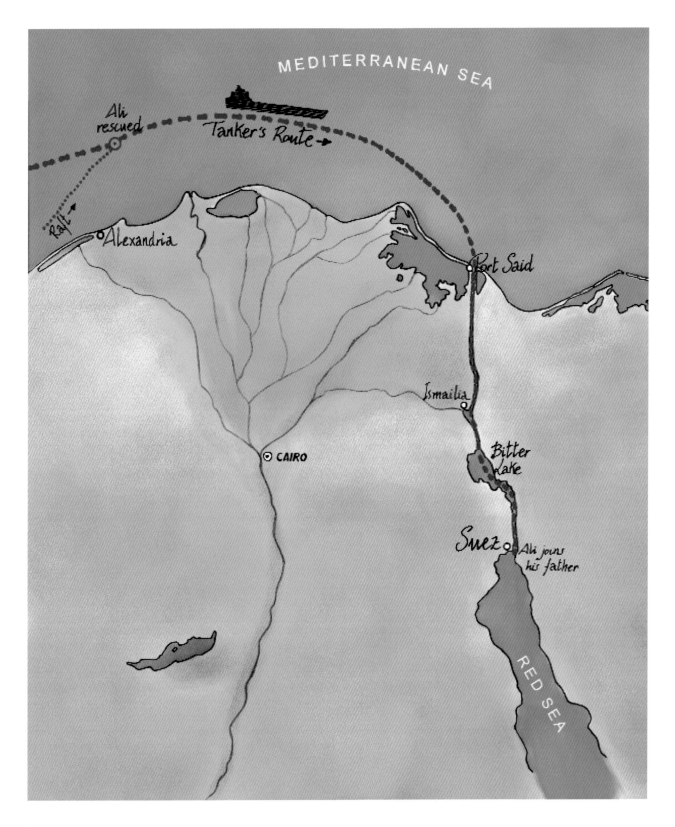

Before long Ali could feel the deep thrum of the engine again, and the tanker began to move. The canal stretched ahead of them, a long ribbon of water forging its way through the desert. Standing so high above the water Ali felt as if he were riding on a great steel beast. On his left, the port side, there was nothing but sand as far as the eye could see, but on the starboard side there were isolated pockets of greenery and the occasional small village. He heard the call to prayer from a mosque as they sailed slowly by and the distant rumble from the railroad on the west bank.

The navigating officer kept a big distance between the *Arabian Star* and the next ship. "So that we have enough time to stop if necessary," the Chief Officer told him. "The last thing anyone wants is a collision."

They passed a dredger digging up the silt from the bottom of the canal. "Why aren't there any locks?" Ali asked. "I thought that canals always had locks." "Good question," the Chief Officer replied. "Do you know what locks do, Ali?" "They change the level of the water, don't they?" Ali said. "Exactly," the Chief Officer replied. "But the Suez Canal joins the sea on both sides. The level of the water in the canal is the same as the level of the water in the Mediterranean Sea and the Red Sea so there is no need for locks."

Ali remained outside on the bridge for a long time. He thought of all the things he might see if he worked on a ship like this. If he were a seaman what job would he do, he wondered. Would he work on the deck or in the engine room or on the bridge? Would he be clever enough to become a Chief Engineer or Chief Officer or even a Captain?

All too soon the Captain called to him, "We're not far from Suez now," he said. Before long Ali could see a tug boat approaching. Several of the crew were disembarking with Ali and the Captain. Ali

said goodbye to the others. They shook his hand and the bosun gave him a hug. He fastened a badge to Ali's overalls. It was a silver star, "For luck," Lester said. In his hand Ali held a bag containing his red T-shirt. That had been lucky too.

It was a long way down to the waiting tug boat. As they chugged away he could see the full extent of the tanker now. It towered above them, dwarfing the little boat. Ali waved to the men standing on the deck growing smaller in the distance. Would he see any of them again, he wondered.

Approaching the quay he could make out a figure peering in their direction. "Ali, is that you?" called a familiar voice. Ali leapt ashore and threw himself into the waiting arms of his father. "You have a fine, brave son," the Captain said. "Keep safe," he said to the boy. Soon now he would see his own son Malik.

Long after the Captain had gone Ali's father held him tight. "I thought I had lost you," he whispered. "Let's go home now, we have a long journey and your mother is waiting."

Early the next morning Ali walked down to the seashore, where only a few days earlier his adventure had begun. It seemed a long time ago. So many things had happened to him in such a short time. Shading his eyes from the sun he could see the shapes of distant ships on the horizon carrying their different cargoes to all the countries in the world. Some of them were probably oil tankers like the *Arabian Star*, he thought. He waved to his father and uncle setting out in their fishing boat.

Turning to go, a sudden movement in the sand caught his eye. As he watched the sand erupted and lots of tiny baby turtles emerged. He picked up one of the hatchlings, it fitted on the palm of his hand. He looked at its tiny head and miniature flippers, it was a perfect copy of a huge adult, he thought. Carrying it carefully to the water's edge, he bent down and released it to the sea.

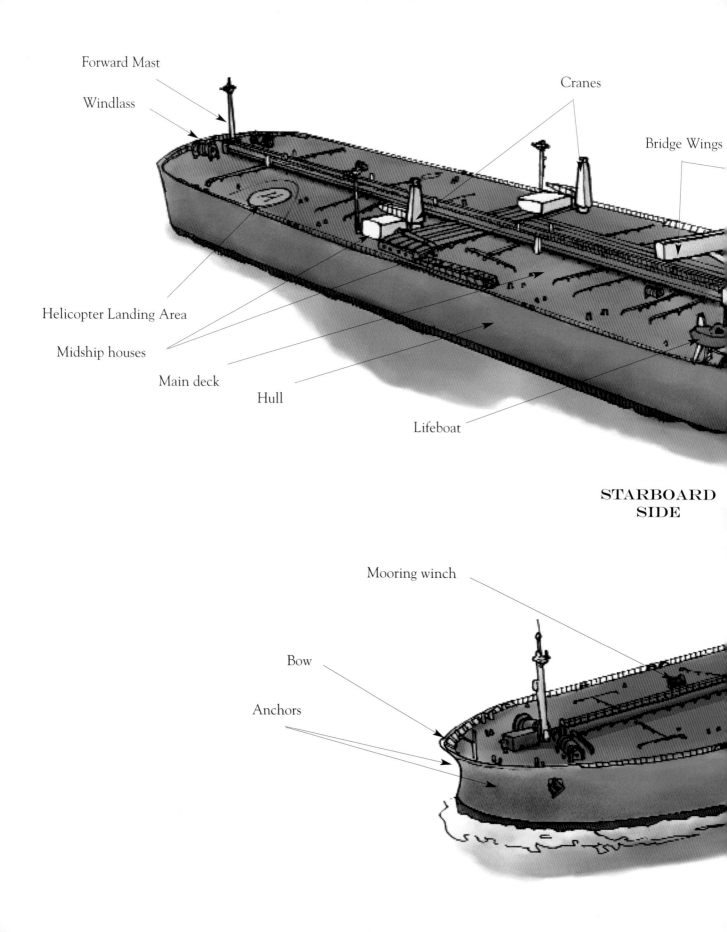

Forward Mast

Windlass

Cranes

Bridge Wings

Helicopter Landing Area

Midship houses

Main deck

Hull

Lifeboat

STARBOARD SIDE

Mooring winch

Bow

Anchors

VESSEL MAIN COMPONENTS

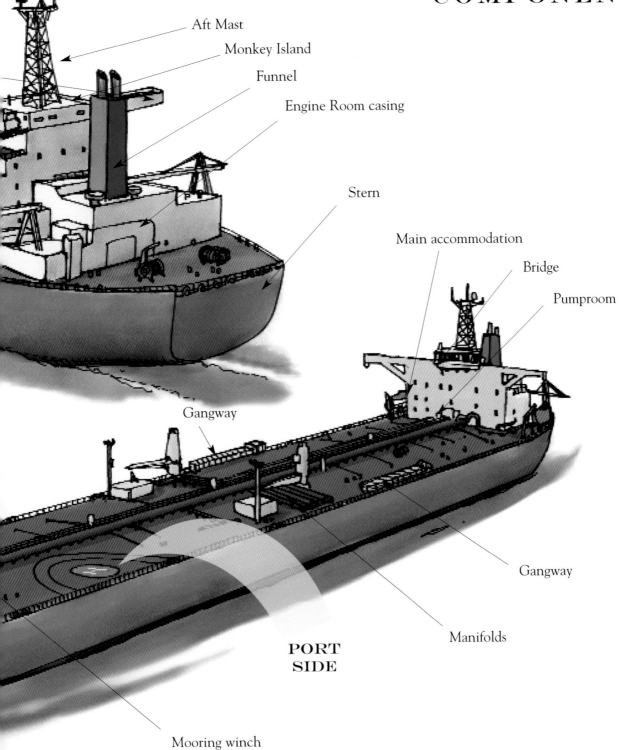

Aft Mast

Monkey Island

Funnel

Engine Room casing

Stern

Main accommodation

Bridge

Pumproom

Gangway

Gangway

Manifolds

PORT SIDE

Mooring winch

Other books by Julia Johnson:

The Pearl Diver
A is for Arabia
One Humpy Grumpy Camel
A Gift of the Sands
Saluki, Hound of the Bedouin
The Cheetah's Tale
The Peacock and the Mermaid

All published by Stacey International
www.stacey-international.co.uk